The Doors of the Church Are

Open

Staying Committed to Christ Even When the Church Fails You©

The Doors of the Church Are Open: Staying Committed to Christ Even When the Church Fails You©

The doors of the church are open, and I need someone to come and rescue me.

The doors of the church are open. I'm in here, but yet I am still not free.

TABLE OF CONTENTS

INTRODUCTION

C hurch attendance is on a steady decline. Why is that, many are asking? Some seem to think Americans are identifying themselves differently when it comes to religion. What does that mean though? I think it means many have embraced the concept of spirituality to mean having a direct relationship with God, and that to go to church and do the weekly routine is to be religious. We see in Matthew 23: 1-4 where Jesus is telling the crowd to "follow the teaching of religious leaders but not the example of them because many of them crush people with unbearable religious demands" (NLT). Many today feel as if church is a religious demand, where you go and are made to feel bad, and you are judged by things that some of those who are judging are guilty of. Many feel as if religious leaders set rules to congregants that they themselves cannot abide by. Is this true? Are the doors of the church open to this type of thing?

Some American Christians are taking a stance and are worshipping in non-traditional ways. In talking to many who feel this way, they feel as if they are considered rebellious, outcasts, backsliders, and unsaved because this is the path they have chosen. I have often asked, can't there be more than one path to the one God? I have yet to receive a direct answer. I am often met with the comment that the book of Hebrews says not to forsake the assembling of ourselves. I agree with all of the Bible; however, if one sentence is not enough to make an essay, and one survey is not enough to gather a true consensus, should one scripture verse be enough to form a doctrine?

I am all for going to church, but I have to ask: How can those of us who believe in a loving God condemn others to hell for finding their own path to that same God? I don't think it makes an individual ungodly; I just think it makes them different. Ungodly is when an individual believes in something other than the one true and living God, Jesus Christ, not when they believe that there is another path to God. What do I mean by path? I mean a spiritual way, a spiritual practice, that does not alter the foundational truths about who Jesus is. For example, if we all agreed that we wanted to meet at a certain restaurant and some of us went by car, some by train, and some by bus does that mean that those who traveled by bus or by train used an invalid means to get themselves there? They arrived safely, on time, and at the same place.

In a *Huffington* Post article titled, "Why Don't We Go To Church Anymore?" by Marc Joseph (2017), the contributing writer gave facts from a Gallup Poll in 2016 that shows the younger generation is turning from religion but say they believe in God. Some of their reasons are: "Religion is too much like a business," "Too many Christians doing un-Christian things," and "Organized religious groups are more divisive than uniting."

What have the doors of the church opened up to? I think it's time to talk about this. The church spends a lot of time criticizing the decline in church attendance with things like: "The younger generation is just crazy," "The younger generation just doesn't want God," "The younger generation just wants to do what they want to do." But how do we defend, how can we criticize, when open doors are walked through, but yet there is still no freedom, there is still no deliverance, there is still no difference in the action they see outside of the church?

This book is not an attack on Christianity. This is about truth. This book is about things I have personally experienced and/or witnessed in the church. This book is about how the church has opened the doors to more than salvation. No, I am not attacking the church as it is the first sense of community I ever found; however, I will not steer away from the truth of what I have experienced and seen. As Christians, we can't continue to say that those who don't want to regularly attend church are just making excuses and really don't want anything to do with God. For too long this has been a line of defense, and it has hindered our ability to witness and win souls.

Every one of us needs hope. The hope that can only be found through Jesus Christ. This book is twofold. I will highlight reasons why people no longer want to associate with the church, and I will highlight reasons why your commitment should be to Jesus Christ and how that will sustain you, even when the church fails you.

CHAPTER 1

"All them hypocrites do is lie, cheat, and steal. I'm not stepping foot in there dead or alive. In fact, when I die y'all can carry my body right over yonder to that community center and eulogize me."

I could hear Mama Mary from outside. I had just walked in the yard and had not even approached the porch, but I could hear her. "Who has stirred her up?" I wondered. Sounds like she is on another one of her church rants.

Before I continue on about Mama Mary, I want to let you know that I am not a church basher. Mama Mary is not denying that she needs hope. She is not declaring that she does not seek daily biblical inspiration. Her rant is based in the fact that the hope she embraced, the hope she put years of trust in, had failed her. There was no way I was going to tell her that a lot of her disappointment was because there was no distinction between trusting in Jesus Christ and trusting in her local church.

Sure, it was more than right for her to have high expectations of her church leaders and members, but not higher than the expectations of the one who established the church. Papa Dee spent many years on the deacon board. He was Pastor's right-hand man. He was so dependable. He would spend some of his Saturdays mowing and maintaining Pastor's yard while his own grass stood knee high.

"You can't tell this fool nothing about his pastor. Here he is at his every beckoning call, but when he was laid off from his job in '74, Pastor never called to see if we even needed a loaf of bread." These were the experiences that Mama Mary just wouldn't let go of. For years she heard about how it would do her good to let it go, and I agreed. Holding on has caused her to be stuck, and ever since Papa Dee passed away, she expressed how unwilling she was to even consider the thought of letting it go.

"Who's gone check him?" She would ask this to everyone who she **thought** was checking her.

This is where we stand in Christianity today. Let's check the congregants but let's pray for the pastor. When it comes down to the things we see and know, not just about the pastor but about any of our church leaders, we are often told not to stir things up or cause any trouble. However, any time anything that is not of God goes unchecked, the things that are open will become contaminated, and thus we have the state of the church today.

Yes, the doors of the church are open. They are open to more than just soul-winning, soul-saving, ministry, and benevolence. They are open to judgement, competition, and elevation of one's own agenda. We need to close the doors on everything that is not like Jesus.

The doors of the church are open, and I need someone to come and rescue me.

The doors of the church are open. I am in here, but yet I am still not free.

CHAPTER 2

"Did y'all hear him get up there and say that he looked out for my husband? The man is lying. I was married to Dee for 47 years. This man did not start Pastoring us until 38 years ago, so I ain't missed nothing. I don't even remember a time when he even gave Dee a ride when our car was broken down."

"Mama Mary, why don't you like Pastor? I think you are being too hard on him. Papa Dee knew how to say no if he didn't want to be doing any of what he did for Pastor."

"Girl look a here! Don't come questioning me about that Pastor. He stands before God's people every Sunday and lie. I have watched him take advantage of my husband and so many others. I don't know what he had on my Dee. It's like Dee was a puppet on a string. And yes, you are so right, Dee did know how to say no....to everybody but his Pastor!"

"Now you know Pastors have a big responsibility. I don't think some people take that into consideration and so they pull the Pastor in too many directions. The expectations are just unrealistic."

"The only direction I have ever wanted to see that Pastor go in was the right direction, but for years I have seen him go in every direction but right. He chose to allow himself to be pulled. He has his own unrealistic expectations of what he should be doing and what he is going to be able to get away with."

"I see."

I wanted to end the conversation right there for now. She is so passionate about how she feels and my duty is to pray for her. I know that if God does not deal with her heart, then these negative feelings about the Pastor and the church will be lasting.

In order to stay committed to Christ, even when we feel as if the church has failed us, we have to understand that there is a distinction between the two. The only reason ungodly things have entered through the doors is because of the lack of commitment to Jesus Christ.

The church is the "body" of Christ, not the "being" of Christ. The love of Jesus and the work of Jesus is demonstrated through His body (the church, the people); however, the body can and should never replace the being or the very existence of Jesus Christ. When there is a misplaced commitment, then it becomes easier to allow people to have the power that causes you to disconnect.

Think about this. If you are employed full time, you spend at the least 40 hours a week with a body (the group of people who make up your team or organization). Very few people will walk out on the being (the existence of) their job because the body disappointed them. Their commitment to that body is such that they will make a career and give 30-40 years of their life to an occupational body but will resign from the body of Christ without even giving a two weeks- notice.

When you are committed to something you defend it, you try to correct it, and you forgive it.

You defend by giving reasons why you are still attached. You also defend by counter-attacking a negative statement with a positive one. If someone says that the company that you work for does not properly pay their employees, you would defend by saying, "but the benefits are good."

You try to correct by giving your input on things that everyone can collectively do to help things get better. You may even provide innovative ideas about the things that can totally be eliminated.

Your commitment won't allow you to quit; rather it invokes you to seek change.

You forgive what or who you are committed to. Although you may have been wronged, you will continue to show up at your job. Even when they keep wronging you, you may continue to show up.

If your job or a person can be defended, attempted to be corrected, and forgiven, then why can't your church body? It's about understanding that the body is a representation of Jesus Christ so to not defend, try to correct, or forgive is a form of rejection to Jesus.

I know that you may say that you can love Jesus and not deal with church people but let me ask you, "how are you being an extension of His unconditional love if you have forsaken the assembly?"

I remember the Sunday that Mama Mary resigned from our church. It wasn't anything formal. I went to pick her up at the usual time. I walked in and she was sitting at the kitchen table with a tall glass of orange juice. She wasn't drinking it. She was gazing into space. She only has her slip on, and the rollers were still in her hair.

"You're not going to church Mama Mary? It's not like you to be half dressed at this time on a Sunday morning. Are you not feeling well?"

"I feel fine sugar. At least my body does. It's my head that's all sick," she said.

"How can I help you? Let's talk about what's really been troubling you? Are you still grieving over Daddy Dee? I would like to put my hand on the issue."

"Sugar you wouldn't understand. There are some things that are best left out of the eyes and ears of your children. Us old folks don't want y'all messed up the way we are. Baby, we have seen some things."

"Mama Mary, I've already seen and heard a lot and it didn't mess me up."

"Chile, you hear me cuss that old insurance man out because he didn't come here and pick up my money for my burial policy on last month, ain't hearing much of nothing. Me throwing that plate away after I swore to Cuttin Gladys that I would eat it, ain't seeing much of nothing. Baby Gladys can't cook, but she always quick to offer someone a plate. I always accept it but no soon as she turns her head I throw it away."

"But Cousin Gladys can cook. She made me breakfast the other day and it was good." I know we were getting off the subject, but Mama Mary brought up Cousin Gladys cooking.

(Mama Mary laughing). Lord-a-mercy, baby Lisa them little boy, the one who just started crawling, can scramble you some eggs and butter you some bread and make that taste good. It doesn't take much in doing that. There's a difference in cooking and just peddling around in the kitchen. That's why me and your mama don't want you fassing around in those streets. Stay under you an older woman who can teach you how to run your house."

I just shook my head.

"You still going to church ain't you Sugar?"

"Yes, Mama Mary."

"Well, you better gone head on but be careful. Keep your eyes open and on the Lord at all times. Don't take any wooden nickels."

"I hear you Mama Mary. I will see you later."

As I drove on to church, I prayed for Mama Mary. I know she has a good heart and I don't want it to be hardened. "Dear God, you know Mama Mary's heart. Please keep it soft. Tap on it so that she will open up, forgive, and free her Pastor and herself. In Jesus name. Amen."

I wonder what is it that Mama Mary knows. I'm not going to dig deep or try to look into it.

I wanted to be more involved at my church. I tried attaching myself to the women groups. I go to the meetings, the luncheons, and the conferences. Slowly but surely, some of the women in the groups prove to be what they are labeled as. I hear the whispering, and the chattering as one woman walks by. Her appearance makes it obvious that she is experiencing some struggles. "At least she's here," I think to myself. I am proud of her for just showing up, despite what she may be going through. I then begin to wonder, "why don't I have the courage to tell her?" She really needed to know that she is being noticed in a good way. Instead, I say nothing, and as expected, I don't see her anymore after a while and the same two who were whispering and chattering about her find a new target.

This target does not appear to know struggle. She is extremely polished, confident, fashionable, and very becoming (as Mama Mary would describe a pretty woman). As she walks by the scent of her perfume is captivating. It lingers. She is now 50 feet away, but the smell of elegance is still there.

Here comes the chatter.

"Her perfume is too loud."

"I would not have worn those color heels with that outfit."

"Her skirt is a little too short for church."

"I didn't like her hair."

Seriously? This was unbelievable. Why not just compliment her? I mean her appearance, demeanor, her walk, and her smile all made it so that one has to get a shovel and have the help of a grave digger, to dig deep to find any flaws. Leave it to Miss Judge and Lady Jurror, THEY.FOUND.SOMETHING.

"Why am I even a part of this women's group?" I started to wonder. Today is my last day. "No, you need to be a part of something bigger than you." I begin to reason with myself. So much so that I started an internal war. It didn't last long though because in walked the ministry leader. She goes straight to the "chatter-two" and asks the question, "Did y'all see Miss Thing? She walked up in here as if she owns this place as if she is the First Lady."

I didn't even wait to hear the response from the other two. It was probably going to be too much for me to listen to. I threw my coat over my right, lower arm, strapped my bag across my left shoulder and out I went.

That door was open to gossip, demeaning, and insulting and I had no intentions of staying behind it. But was leaving the right thing to do? I don't think there is a right or a wrong answer. It's an opinion, maybe even a judgement call. It did cause me to question my own commitment to Christ because I allowed gossip to run me away from something that I might have just had the potential to impact and influence.

I didn't even stay for the second service like I usually do.

You know Mama Mary had a field day when I called her. I could hear the excitement in her voice as she reminded me of her words to me over 2 months ago.

Her words were, "he's infecting everything in the church. He's a fool, he's married to a fool, he was appointed to by a bunch of fools, and he is leading a flock of fools. I'm done with it all. I ain't no fool."

She had such a way with words. Even if they weren't the right words, they would marinate on your mind, become digestible, and even had the potential to be regurgitated and repeated, if you were angry enough at someone.

I told Mama Mary that there is a lot of good in Pastor. I talked about all of the ministries that he has started within our church and about how he makes sure we do our part in the community. She said she expected more. I asked her what is the more that she expected. Her reply was, "Baby the things that I expect of him can't be seen. I expect a pure heart; I expect clean hands; I even expect an apology."

I don't know what she wanted an apology for other than him overworking Papa Dee. I hoped that she finds the strength to forgive, move forward, and be okay with an apology that she may never receive. Whatever she needed one for anyway.

Chapter Highlights:

The church congregation is made up of a bunch of flawed individuals. There are certain standards that Christians must uphold. The denomination as a whole is judged when one of us stumbles or falls. For this reason, integrity, honesty, repentance, and holiness is a must.

The hardest thing about being a Christian is that once people know that you are, you are no longer allowed to be human. There is no space for error. The expectations are not realistic. Human assumptions of expectations are where we are divided. Just as Jesus experienced frustrated and angry crowds, persecution, and even crucifixion when He did not meet the unrealistic expectations of mankind, so will we.

Do what you know to do and never allow man's opinion to replace God's instructions.

CHAPTER 3

J ulie was very reserved. She was 22 years old. She wasn't in school, but she was working. She had 2 children already. There was this sadness that was always in her eyes. She faithfully came to church, but she didn't mingle much. After the benediction, she would grab her children up and out the door they would go. I never saw anyone reach out to her. I guess I was the only one who saw the sadness in her eyes. This bothered me, so I went and spoke to the Deaconess about it. I knew that once these elder women became aware they would do as instructed in Titus 2, they would take her under their wings. They would get her all cheered up.

That following Sunday after church I walked into the Deaconess meeting room and I had a conversation with Linda about Julie. Linda looked at me and said, "Baby if she needs us she knows where to find us. We are way too busy making sure the Sunday service and the kitchen is run right. We can't run nobody down."

"Was she serious?" I thought.

In chimed Rebecca. "Yeah, she knows how to open her mouth. If she's sad, it's probably because her children's daddy is back running behind that girl that lives across town. If she let him be, she'll be fine."

I heard enough. What if that wasn't her case? What if it was something deeper than her children's father and who he is running around with? And they are quick to holler, "let them call for the elders of the church."

"Okay fine, forget I ever said anything. I just thought. Never mind."

"You thought what?' asked Rebecca. "Don't you get like that Pastor of ours. Always saying he thought this and he thought that when he already knew how things are."

"Good day Rebecca," I replied.

I walked out. There was too much ego in that room. Julie needs help, but they are too important to reach out to her. They require that she reach out to them, something that she may never do, but their egos won't allow them to see that.

I made up in my mind that I was going to break the ice with Julie on next Sunday. And I did.

I got up and walked out of the church shortly before the benediction on that following Sunday. Sure enough, immediately after the benediction was given, out came Julie and her two children. They were walking fast. You would have thought someone was after them. Well, I was....sort of.

"Hello Julie, how are you?'

"I am okay. I'm trying to get home."

"Are you walking?"

"Yes, I am, but I am used to it. Enjoy the rest of your Sunday" said Julie.

You're not getting rid of me so easily I thought. Now since she said she was walking, I allowed my nosiness to kick in. Of course, I wanted to know how far of a walk she had.

"Julie, I hate to see you walking with your babies. I'd be more than.."

"No, no, no." She cut me off. "We are fine. Thank you."

She cut that short. However, I was determined to get next to her to see if I can help her. I had forfeited too many opportunities to make a difference in the lives of others and I just didn't want to do this with Julie. I will find another approach. It will be one with caution. I won't be too pushy for fear that if I am too pushy, I may drive her away from me and the church. I thought about the bible verse that said, "he who wins souls is wise." I wanted to win this soul and I knew I had to be wise about it.

When our egos get in the way, we lose people instead of winning them over. We become so anxious to clean a fish before we catch it. We have them on the hook, but before we are able to reel them in, we say or do something that cause them to slip from our grasp. Over the years I have seen so many slip from the grasp of the Just Jesus Ministry. We didn't always lose them because they didn't love God. We lose people due to lack of empathy, lack of compassion, and lack of spiritual service. We think that catching the fish is inviting them to church, but because there is a steady decline in church attendance and because people have made up in their mind that they will not come to church, we must invite them to Jesus and then clean them up at church. I have always been taught the opposite. Catch them by having them come to church and clean them by getting them to accept Jesus. What if they never come to church? I say catch them by getting them to accept Jesus and the church will groom and clean them if they decide to come. If they find a place, they can trust. If they can get cleansed without their dirtiness being judged first.

Think about the times you have changed cell phone carriers, medical doctors, careers, or even cars. You changed because there was a need that went unmet. Your expectations may not have been met. Even when a church makes a change for the better, they will still lose some people because sometimes the changes does not meet the needs of those you once had in your grasp.

Empathy is described as putting yourself in another situation and feeling the emotion that they are feeling. For example, the grip was lost on Susan when she became unemployed and went through financial hardship. Susan wholeheartedly believed in tithing, and she did it faithfully. Imagine the disappointment that she experienced when she went to the benevolent committee and was turned away. Mama Mary was just as, if not more than, disappointed. I regret that I went home and told her about it.

"Mama Mary, do you remember Susan?"

"Which Susan, sugar? Johnny's Susan or Martha them baby Susan?" She asked me.

"Ms. Martha's Susan."

"Yes, I remember Susan. She has been on the Usher Board for years. She also worked over 20 years at the plant before they had that big lay-off."

"Yes, that's her. She went up to the altar today. They gave her the mic and asked if she would like to share her prayer request with the church. She said her spirit wasn't right and some things in this ministry wasn't right. Here's what she said:"

19

"As most of you all know I have been a member here for 39 years. Since I was ten years old. I have always believed in tithes and offerings. I started tithing 22 years ago and never missed an opportunity. I've kept every transaction, and it has totaled $173,400 just in tithes. I've probably given another $100,000 in offerings. I didn't keep count on my offerings. I received a severance package when I was laid off from my job. I paid bills off with that money and of course, I gave money to the church. A month came when I didn't have money for groceries so I came to the benevolent ministry and they wrote me a check for $200. I was so appreciative. I started doing some part-time work at Wal-Mart to make ends meet, but about 2 months later I was short on a bill. I needed $300 for my light bill. This committee right here (pointing her finger) that calls themselves the benevolent committee told me that it was too soon for them to help me again. They said I could only receive assistance once a year. To make matters worse, Sister Quarles looked me in my face and said that I should have managed my severance pay better. How benevolent is that? I walked out on them because I knew the Holy Ghost didn't have a good grip on my tongue or my hands after she said that. I forgave Sister Quarles, but I stand here today to say that this will be my last Sunday here. I wanted to make peace before I leave and I want to give this check for $200. This is the money back that y'all gave to me. The bible says, "Owe no man anything but to love him, and I want to obey the Bible." I appreciate what y'all did for me. I really do; however, it's disheartening to know that what you support won't support you back. I gave tithes in good faith. I didn't have to be obedient to the word, like so many others aren't, but I chose to do what I know would benefit others. Sister Quarles, I pray that you never find yourself in a situation like mine. I want to see all of y'all blessed."

Mama Mary replied, "I'm glad she said it. It needed to be said. What did the Pastor say?"

"He stood up and thanked her for coming up, and he apologized for her church experience. He then said that effectively immediately all altar prayer will be handled in the back. You can come down for prayer and an intercessor will take you to the back and pray with you."

That's just like him. He tries to cover up everything" said Mama Mary.

"Well Mama Mary, when we give our tithes and offerings, we are doing it as unto the Lord and I don't think we should be bringing that back up. I agree that they could have been a little more considerate to someone who has been as faithful in her giving as Susan, but I don't think her response to it was right."

Mama Mary looked at me in disbelief. "Girl I'll drag you out of that church before I let them brainwash you. It seems as if you are on their defense when someone points out their wrongs."

I understand ow Mama Mary could feel that way. I really do. I'm not trying to cover up anything that has gone wrong at the church; however I certainly don't want to be one who is spreading the gossip, spilling any tea, or posting the pain. I am committed to Christ. The church is His body. There are things that I don't like about my own physical body, but you won't catch me doing any harm to it. That's how I feel about my church. There are things that I don't like about my church body, but I'm for sure not going to slander and cause any verbal harm to it.

We are making a voluntary choice when we join a church. We tend to say that God led us to a certain ministry, but it's still a voluntary choice to obey the voice of God. To defend your church is to defend your choice. Here are three reasons why you should defend your church:

1. To defend the church is to defend Jesus Christ. This does not mean that things that are not like Jesus does not enter through the doors of the church. It simply means that because the church is His body, we should want to protect it

2. To defend the church is to defend your faith. It's your faith in the church's ability to restore, heal, and to help through the power of Jesus Christ. When you don't

defend the church, you are saying that you are not confident in its ability to do those things.

3. To defend your church is to defend humanity. Your defense of the church does not mean that you are making a false claim that the church is perfect. Instead, your defense of the church is saying that you believe in the power of Jesus Christ and in His ability to help humanity live in the power of His resurrection.

I'm not sure if my responses to Mama Mary were considered defending the church, but I am so committed to Christ, so I don't take back any of them. It doesn't mean that I agree with everything that goes on in the church. It just means that my commitment anchors me. I'm not going to be so quick to bail out.

Mama Mary has never asked me to stop going to church. It just seems as if she wants me to guard myself. I think I am already doing that especially since I walked away from the women's ministry. However, I do often wonder if I should have stayed and tried to make a difference. Sometimes my internal voice tells me that had I stayed it's possible that I would have seen or heard something that would have been too much for my spirit and would have led me to leaving the church. Just because it's going on in the church and has God's name attached to it does not that you should be a part of it. A good thing is not always a God thing. It's always okay to want to be connected to people and things that are conducive to our spiritual growth. You can remain in a church and not be a part of certain ministries. It's being out of total fellowship that questions our commitment.

I begin to think about Julie. I sure want to cover more ground with her on Sunday. I should pray about it and ask the Holy Spirit to lead me. Anytime we are trying to witness to someone; we must use prayer and the guidance of the Holy Spirit as our strategy.

That would be my strategy with Julie. I know that she attends church, but she is so disconnected. I want to be her connection. I want her to know that she doesn't have to be a part of a certain church clique in order to find a friend. I was willing to be friends with her.

Many Christians have a strategy for witnessing to those who haven't accepted Jesus and that's very important. However, it is equally important to witness to those who have accepted Jesus Christ, are in church, but feel alone. We shouldn't forget about them, yet we often do.

We put so much emphasis on getting them in the door and then we let them bear the burden of trying to figure out what's and connecting. We should be evangelizing those in the church.

When you invite someone to your house, they don't assume that they can just go to your refrigerator and fix themselves something to drink. They want to feel welcomed to do that. Such it is with the church. We invite people in, but we don't make them feel welcome to connect.

I know it is the Holy Spirit who is leading me to Julie. Whenever we witness, and to whomever we witness to, it must be Spirit-led. When it is not, we have the tendency to say the wrong thing and scare people off. I'm praying for the next opportunity to find out why Julie does not connect with anyone at church. In my prayer, I am asking God to show her my heart so that she will know that I am sincere. I think this should become a universal prayer for all disciples of Jesus Christ. Sometimes people have shut down because when they did open it, there was no sincerity.

I will be authentic the next time I speak to Julie. There's no way I am going to try to impress her by telling her about the things that I don't do. I will simply share with her how much Jesus loves her and how much He wants her to be connected to other like-minded believers.

That's my witnessing strategy:

    (a) To be Spirit-led
    (b) To be prayerful
    (c) To be authentic

I think I will call Mama Mary and share this with her.

Chapter Highlights:

Evangelism is a vital part of the Christian faith. It's important because eternity in hell is at stake for so many. We ourselves must get rid of the religious routine of being so spiritually high on Sunday's but be on a spiritual decline the rest of the week. Our lives, our very presence should minister to people.

Evangelism is two-fold. We lift Jesus up before people, and then we help make disciples of them after they accept Him as Lord and Savior. We have mastered lifting Him up before them. We know exactly what to say to get people to come to church; however, we are not making great witnesses once they get in and therefore we fail to make disciples.

Spirit-Led: The Holy Spirit will lead you to the person to whom He wants you to witness to. Stay consecrated and in tune to His voice so that you are clear on WHO you should approach.

Prayerful: As you communicate with God, He will tell you WHAT to say. The words that He will give you will lift Jesus up, and it's His job to draw the person who you are witnessing to. Prayer is important because so often we try to do the drawing. For this reason, we experience overwhelm and become weary in our well-doing. We were never given the responsibility to draw others. John 12:32 (KJV) says, "And I, if I be lifted up from the earth, will draw all men unto me." As we prayerfully communicate with others they should see Jesus above everyone and everything else. When they do, they are will be drawn by His power and His love.

Authentic: Why would anyone want to serve God, want to go to church, or any of that if the people who are witnessing to them are coming across as perfect and judgmental. It's okay to be a work in progress. We all are. This does not mean that you should open your skeletal closet and tell people all of your short-comings. After all, this could be a turn-off. However, you should let people know that Jesus did not find you in a synagogue praying seven times a day, speaking in tongues, feeding the poor, and baptizing saints. You found Him when you needed a Savior and His unconditional love and forgiveness captured you.

Pamela D. Smith

CHAPTER 4

I sure did miss having Mama Mary go to church with me every Sunday. I wasn't going to be pushy, but I sure was not going to give up. At times, I felt as if there is so much weight on my shoulder, seems as if I am the one who always try to have people to commit. Mama Mary has always stood form on the fact that she is committed to Christ and it does not take going to church, being around a bunch of people who weren't, in order to prove it. I have always stood firm on the fact that a commitment to Christ is evident in how well we take care of His body.

Whenever I say that to Mama Mary her response is always, "the body of Christ should take care of you and make you want to keep taking care of it but now days the church just wants us to give money and all of our time and then when you need them there are all kinds of restrictions. That's not a true body of Christ."

I would never reply back to that. Not because I didn't have any thoughts, but because I always used wisdom. Wisdom will not allow one to walk into a fight not knowing what ammunition the opposing party has. Mama Mary always has some kind of ammunition that would back you up in a corner and leave you defenseless.

Sunday came. I decided to sit on the same row that Julie and her children always sat on. I was there early. I had Ritz crackers in my purse. I wanted to make sure I had something to offer her children if they became restless. This would be a way to break ice with Julie. At least I hoped. I was all prayed up.

Julie and her children came in right at the start of service. The children appeared to be well behaved because they took their seats hurriedly. They didn't do much scrambling around like I see lots of kids do. Julie never looked over at me during praise and worship. I kept my eyes on her though. Every time the worship leader would say, "turn and look at your neighbor," I didn't have to turn because I was already looking at her. I was trying to read her, trying to assign meaning to her facial expressions and her body language. She made it very difficult.

I noticed that Julie bowed her head as if she was praying when it was Pastor's time to get up and preach. That's excellent I thought until I saw her pull out a pair of ear plugs. I was puzzled. Why was she sitting in church every Sunday but tuning out the sermon? I definitely had to get her to open up to me, or somebody, at this point. Before Pastor gave his reference scripture for his sermon Julie had already opened her Bible and appeared to be diligently reading. I was so curious. I wanted to slide a note over to her and literally beg her to tell me what was this all about. Instead, I held my curiosity.

I don't remember what scripture Pastor gave as a reference because I was so engaged in watching Julie. About this time, her kids became anxious. I almost hugged them for becoming anxious because now I get to say something to Julie.

"Do you think a snack will help? I have some Ritz crackers."

"Sure," Julie replied.

The smiles that lit up on their face when I handed them the Ritz. I could tell that Julie was relieved. She stood up and thanked me after the benediction. She claimed that was the first time anyone at church had done anything nice for her and her children. It was unbelievable. How does one go to church and find that having nice things done or said is scarce? Is it because the doors are now open to that? Is it because those in leadership are so busy trying to grow the membership that they have stopped trying to grow those who are already there? What happened to fellowship and hospitality? Did that stuff creep out the door as the other stuff crept in?

I offered Julie and her children a ride again and of course, she turned me down. I really thought that this would be the Sunday that I connected with her. Oh well, at least I was one step closer.

I headed to Mama Mary's. This was second Sunday and every second Sunday she cooked pot roast. Her cooking schedule was embedded in my brain. She could make a gravy thicker than the fog in San Francisco. I could smell the pot roast when I opened my car door! I walked in and gave her a kiss on the cheek. She looked at me and smirked.

"You ole faithful you," she said.

"Why are you calling me that? Is it because I attend church as much as I can?" I asked.

"Yes, that's exactly it. But you know baby I like that and I know that you've been praying for me because these last few weeks I have been sitting 'round here with a vexed spirit. I ain't had a bit of business trying to poison your mind against the church. I've seen the hop that place has given you. You walk 'round here with so much joy and peace. You could be running 'round here like Felisha's daughter. Every time I see that poor girl walk by here I get troubled because I know she is troubled. You ought to stop by there one Sunday and invite her to church with you. Just tell her to be careful because a person can go there for healing and end up hurt."

"Mama Mary I am sure glad that I stopped by today. I wouldn't have wanted to miss hearing you say what you're saying. You have been in my prayers and this is confirmation that God hears me."

"Chile, you know He hears you. You have such a clean heart and such a right spirit. I'm proud to see that you are so committed to Christ that you don't pay me no mind when I get to talking about that church of ours."

"I listen when you speak Mama Mary. It's just that I have learned to filter information. I hold on to what applies to me, and I disregard what doesn't. My decision can't be based on your experience, and I'm glad that you are not mad at me for that."

"Just listen at you sounding wise and all. There's no way I could be mad at you for that. Ain't nothing foolish about me."

"I had a chance to sit with Julie and her children today. We had a small conversation. I really would like to get to know her better."

"I'll always caution you because I love you. Don't get tangled up with nobody who's going to contaminate your spirit. Some folks you have to love from a distance. Julie walks around quiet, but she's doing some talking. She's talking around with these men in town. In fact, she's doing a heap more than talking with 'em. That's why her lips so tight when she come 'round some women. She can't say whose children those are because they belong to somebody's husband. I think it's the Pastor. I'm not going to get into that right now, but my heart is set on it. I think she is the scandal that I haven't been able to put my finger on.

Now I hate that I had not headed to the kitchen sooner. I think what Mama Mary just said may have put a little contamination in my spirit. Lord have mercy. Is this why Julie put on her earplugs while Pastor was preaching? I had to catch myself. I am not going there. I am not going to create a story in my mind that may not be true. That is not fair and if I am going to get close to Julie, I had to be fair.

"Let's go eat Mama Mary. That's why I came, to eat with you."

"That means it's time for me to shut my mouth. I hear you chile." Mama Mary said with laughter.

Mama Mary always was keen on clues. The rest of my time spent with her that day went good. We didn't say anything else about church or any of the people at church. I was so anxious to get back next Sunday. I had made Julie my assignment and she didn't feel as if I was doing anything wrong. That's the responsibility of a child of God, to find other children and embrace and love them back to our Father.

Throughout the week, I made sure that I was conscious of what I said, did, and how I acted. I even paid attention to the things that I liked and shared on social media. A social media like and share is a confirmation of approval, so I did not want to like or share anything that was contrary to who I am in Christ. Although I have a spiritual ritual that I have followed for years, although I have set times that I pray throughout the day, although I fast three days every month, none of these things proved my commitment to Christ. Sure it meant that I had some discipline but being disciplined in some areas does not prove commitment.

I was disciplined in going to church every Sunday that I could.

I was disciplined in attending weekly bible study.

I was disciplined in paying my tithes.

I was disciplined in serving in a ministry.

The commitment is shown in the way I love others as He has commanded me. The way I treat others who are not in my clique. The way I forgive others. My willingness to reach out to others and minister life into them without getting any credit, recognition, or money.

I've seen the doors of the church open to things that should have never gone on or gone wrong in the church. I have seen leaders fail because they were not giving themselves over to prayer and fasting like they should. I've seen leaders get elevated and become cocky and preach arrogant messages. I've seen the administration of the church get so caught up in the business and benefits that they forgot about benevolence. Faithful tithe payers being charged for things that should be free. I've been looked at wrong, talked to harshly, ignored, looked over, and misused.................IN THE CHURCH. Honestly, some of this stuff I've never even experienced in the world. I remained committed to Christ and that commitment keeps me connected to the church.

Chapter Highlight:

Church hurt is real. There is no denying it. It's not fair to tell a person to just get over it. Instead, solutions need to be offered to help them heal. A church whose doors are only open to the things of Jesus will help with the healing. This does not mean that there is a perfect church, but it does mean that there should be less errors and less of the blatant, obvious mistreatment of members and visitors. We can't expect perfection from a church that is made up of imperfect humans but what we should expect is accountability. In every church there will be issues that need to be resolved and a Christ centered church will be willing to resolve those issues. A Christ-centered church does not try to cover up the issues and shut down or sit down the person who is calling the issue out.

CHAPTER 5

Sunday came and I was full of joy. I was looking forward to trying again with Julie. I had been praying for months about it. I was going to get there early again. As I was getting dressed, I begin to ask God to give me the words to say. I grabbed Ritz crackers on my way out the door. I wanted to make sure I had something to offer her kids again.

When I got to church Julie and her kids were already there. I walked in and to my surprise, Julie beckoned for me. I sat down on the opposite end of Julie; the kids were in between us. Julie seemed to be very happy this Sunday. She still did not listen to the sermon. She pulled her earplugs out again when Pastor started preaching. My curiosity was sure enough running wild now. At offering time, Julie passed me a note. The note asked if I would be willing to give her and her children a ride home from church. Would I? If only she knew. This is what I have been waiting for. This would be my chance to really build some rapport with her.

After service, Julie and her children walked to the car with me. The children were excited about not having to walk home today. As I begin to crank the car I offered to stop anywhere else Julie may need to go.

"No thank you. I just really appreciate you for giving us a ride home. If you have time, I'd like to get my kids settled and then talk to you." Julie said.

"Time? Yes, I have it." I replied.

Julie directed me to her house. As I pulled into the driveway, I could tell that the inside was cozy. The scent of the country apple candle that she left burning seeped through the door.

"Come on in and have a seat please. I'll just fix their plates and be right back with you. May I fix you something to drink?"

"Water is fine," I replied. She didn't know she had already given me a cup of joy.

This was an answered prayer.

I think Julie had cooked meatloaf because there was a pleasant smell of bell peppers and tomato sauce.

I noticed that Julie had on her house slippers when she returned to the living room. This meant that we would be having an enriching conversation because she was comfortable.

She walked over to me and extended her hand. "I'm Julie Thomas. We've never officially met."

"I'm Loretta Spencer. It's such a blessing to officially meet and to receive an invitation into your home."

"Thank you for accepting the invitation. I know that you've been trying to get close to me and talk for a while now." I was stunned. I wondered how she figured it out. I guess it wasn't hard to though.

"How'd you know that?" I asked.

"I have a prayer life and God showed me that you were. He showed me the sincerity of your heart," she answered.

Amazing, I thought. That's just like God. After all, that is what I prayed for. "Is that what made you open up to me?" I asked. "You know you were being pretty short with me for months. I know you didn't mean it, so I never took offense to it."

"I had to try the spirit by the spirit. I had to make sure that us connecting would be of God. I opened up before and experienced so much hurt. After my last experience, I asked God to give me a spirit of discernment and He did. Some of the people who tried to reach out to me before you just weren't genuine and God showed me that. I'm thankful that I have patience and I am willing to listen to Him and wait on Him. God showed me through my last hurtful experience that I am to love everyone, but that does not mean that I should let everyone into my space.

"I definitely understand that. I am definitely guarded."

"So, let's talk. What is it that you would like to know?" Julie asked me.

"Are you happy? I've watched you Sunday after Sunday attend service and then quickly vanish, not socializing, not hanging around to mingle. Where is your family?"

"To be honest, there are Sundays that I come to church that I am unhappy. Life happens to everyone and we don't have to like it; however, the joy of the Lord is so deep in my soul until I just keep on keeping on. As far as my family, my mother's side all have pretty much went back to Louisiana, but my father's family is still here in the area. We just don't don't interact."

"May I ask why?"

"The doors of the church opened up so wide on me. I was hurt and I did things to hurt someone else. I was right where I should have gotten healed, but no-one wanted to have anything to do with me. The problem with church people is that they put a weight on sin. If it's not what they have been guilty of, then they think it weighs heavier than the things they are guilty of."

"I'm so sorry Julie. I hate to hear that you had that kind of experience in the church."

"It was pretty bad. The only thing that I hate is that I hurt a family and disappointed a lot of others as a result. I was working in the church until the mistreatment became so bad that I had to resign."

I begin to think about what Mama Mary said and without giving it a second thought I asked, "Did Pastor Johnson hurt you?"

Julie sighed. It was a sigh of relief and not one of agitation. "Finally, someone asks me that. Everyone else who questions me always ask me what did I do to him. Why did I make him disown me? Pastor Johnson is my father?"

"Your fa... Your father? I was getting choked up. Is this why you don't listen when he preaches?"

"Correct. It's hard to listen to him give good news when his treatment of me was so bad. It's hard to see and hear him talk of forgiveness when he hasn't forgiven me."

"Why even come to church then Julie?"

"I vowed to stay committed to Christ although the church failed me. If you have a little time, I would like to tell you why it's important to stay committed to Christ even when the church fails you. The doors of the church should remain open, but it needs to be open to the right things.

My mother and Pastor Johnson had an affair before Pastor Johnson was married. Once he got married, his wife never accepted me. She wanted to have this perfect image and didn't want anyone interfering with their lives. Pastor Johnson never acknowledged me publicly. I went to school with his other children and it offended them when schoolmates would call us brothers and sisters. In their mind, the schoolmates were calling their Father a liar. He said I wasn't his child and their father had no reason to lie. After all, he was a Pastor. His mother, his sisters and brothers all wanted me to be a part of their family so bad. They went out of their way to welcome me. I wanted to let them know that this wasn't their fault. They didn't have to try to make up where he never tried to step up."

"Julie, I don't know what to say. As long as I've been going to that church, I have never heard any word about this."

"Loretta, if you notice Pastor Johnson has surrounded himself with people who don't challenge him, with people who are stunting his growth. From what I understand, he asked them years ago not to make mention of this. It was obvious that his wife's happiness an image was more important than his daughter's well-being. I empowered the secret. When I turned twelve, he would call once or twice a year, and during our conversations, he would tell me about how his wife was having a hard time accepting me and how he wanted me to understand and give it time."

"So, Julie let me get this straight. He was asking a child to be an adult about the situation while allowing the adult to act like a child?"

"You are absolutely right, Loretta. I was expected to understand how she felt, but I don't think she was being asked to understand how I must have felt."

"That's awful. In fact, it's one of the most hurtful things I've heard coming from the church."

"Well the reason I kept going to church is because I know that there is no failure in God. I prayed and prayed and God healed my heart of that pain. I truly believe that the only reason. He did was because I remained faithful because I stayed committed to Him."

"You are right. I always tell people to pray for those who despitefully use and mistreat them. They may get by, but they never get away. God is all-knowing."

"Prayed I did. I would be so embarrassed when people who knew that he was my father would tell me things about him that I should have known as his child. He taught for years at the University and classmates would come and ask me if I could put a word into him for them. It was heartbreaking because I knew that

I had to way to contact him, even if I really needed to. Honestly, I think it still hurts today. I have forgiven him, but that does not always immediately take the pain away. Does that make sense?"

"Yes, it does make sense Julie. I do think that it is possible to be walking in forgiveness yet in pain. Forgiveness is not an eraser and forgiving someone does not mean that you get amnesia. It just means that you are no longer holding anything against that person. The process of being healed of the pain takes time. You have to see him embrace other people children every Sunday. I can't imagine how hard that must be."

"I continue to come to church because I don't want my children to feel the brokenness that I feel. Every Sunday I tell them that we are going to hear granddaddy talk about Jesus. I also tell them that granddaddy is going to be so busy afterwards and we can't disturb him. I wouldn't dare want them to think that he just doesn't want to have anything to do with us."

"What about when they get older Julie? What will you tell them then? They may try to reach out to him on their own. Do you think you may be setting them up for a heartbreak if he doesn't receive them well?'

"My faith says no, Loretta. Jesus loves them is all I keep telling myself. His love for them is going to soften Pastor Johnson's heart towards them."

"Such great faith you have. I admire it."

"Loretta if you don't mind me asking, how old are you?"

"I'm 43."

"43? You are the same age as another alleged sister of ours. I've never met her though. I don't think his other children have either. I guess his absence never bothered her because I have never heard of her coming forth."

"Wow. He sounds as if he may have been a rolling stone."

"Well, me and her were both before his marriage and his ministry; however, somehow he managed to put us last."

"I'm so sorry, but if it will help you feel any better Julie, I've never met my father. My mom nor my grandmother have never told me anything about him. I was raised such that I never questioned them about it. I'm too afraid they will consider it disrespectful. They always tell me that I have four fathers: God, my grandfather, and them both. I just let that be."

"I understand that you don't want to be disrespectful, but I think you deserve to know. Or let me ask you, do you want to know?"

"I'm not sure I do," I replied. Julie had put something on my mind that I don't think has ever been on it. Do I want to know? I wondered if it would do me any good to know.

Julie: "I really saw an ugly side to the church when I graduated college. Things weren't as easy as they made it seem while they are encouraging you to go to college. I expected to have a job waiting on me once I graduated. That didn't happen. It came to a point where I needed money to pay my bills. My mom had moved back to Ruston, Louisiana and I just didn't want to go back there. Instead, I started dating an older man. The community called him a sugar daddy. I was drawn to him because the little girl in me was yearning for her father. This relationship added shame on top of the shame that I felt from being disowned by my father. The church folks talked about me. A lot of it was too my face. To this day, a lot of them still won't have anything to do with me. That's why you never see me interacting at church. I believe in giving people their space while praying for their hearts. I cried many nights after that relationship ended. The things that I felt about myself caused me to suffer from depression. Two children were born from that unfruitful relationship."

"God didn't love you any less, Julie. You knew that right?'

"I know it now, but back then I thought God had forsaken me and that He didn't want to have anything else to do with me. In my mind, since the church is the bride of Christ and this is how they were treating me then surely this must be how God feels about me. It was years later when the scripture, "I will never leave you nor forsake you" begin to minister to me. I had to remind myself of that scripture so many times."

"Were you hurt because the relationship ended?"

"No, I was hurt because I allowed it to last so long. I was hurt because my absent father syndrome caused me to be careless and resulted in me hurting a wife and possibly a family. I was hurt because two innocent children were born and had to have a secret love affair with their father because of my carelessness. God forgave me, but I had such a hard time forgiving myself."

"I know that self-forgiveness is hard, but we have to remember to separate the person from the act and then we have to detach from the negative emotions associated with the act."

"I wish I had you to talk to back then Loretta. Your spirit is so calming and your words are so encouraging."

"That's how every disciple of Jesus Christ should strive to be. We can't say we love Him and withhold love from His children. Do you have plans to reach out to your father?"

"I am still praying about it. I want it to be a peaceful encounter. I don't want to get my feelings hurt."

"I actually think you have inspired me to have a conversation with my mother and grandmother. I am going to be strong and courageous."

"Good for you. I want to invite you back over again on next Sunday. I want you to plan to eat dinner with me and my children."

"I would really love that Julie. I look forward to it. Y'all enjoy the rest of the day."

I walked out of Julie's house feeling accomplished. I feel as if I have extended a hand to her and now she has someone who she can talk to and not be judged.

I got in my car and headed to Mama Mary's. I was excited to tell her that I had engaged in real ministry today. I opened myself up to someone who the church had isolated. I didn't have to give a bunch of scriptures; there was no pointing out her faults; there was no laying on of hands. Don't get me wrong, all of that has it's place, but I extended the love of Jesus without judgement or conditions. That's the only thing that the doors of the church should be open to.

I called my mom and asked her if she could come over to Mama Mary's. She said she was already there and was wondering why I had not been by yet. I told her where I had been and advised that I would be pulling up in a few minutes.

48

I could not hear the sound of the television as I approached the porch. Usually Mama Mary has the television up very loud. She swears that she doesn't enjoy the program if it's not turned up loud.

I walked in and noticed that Mama Mary looked disturbed. I looked over at my mama and her countenances was also puzzling. I'm now wondering what has gone wrong. I waited a few minutes to see if either of them would offer any information as to why they were looking like that.

After several minutes of silence, my mom asked if I was going to eat. I told her yes, but it would be after they tell me whatever it is that they need to tell me.

Mama Mary sighed, "Janice ain't no sense in beating 'round the bush with this girl. Lord knows it's time. Me and you both done been quiet far too long."

My Mom: "Loretta, we both got a call from someone at the church. They wanted us to know that Julie and her children were seen getting in the car with you."

Me: "And?"

My Mom: "And, it's time that I let you know that Julie is your sister."

My mom hesitated on the sister part. I felt hot. I felt faint. Let me sit before I fall.

"Say what now? So, who is my father? You mean to tell me.....?"

My Mom: "Yes, baby. Pastor Johnson is your father. I'm sorry that I waited so long to tell you. Him and I had a relationship before he started preaching and long before he was married. Mom and Dad never liked him because they felt as if he should have married me after I became pregnant. They wouldn't let him come around and have anything to do with either of us. Once he started preaching and was appointed as the Pastor of our church, I stopped attending. Papa Dee was already a deacon there, so they eventually developed a relationship. Papa Dee could be spiteful at times, so he didn't forgive him until af......"

Mama Mary cut her off quick. "Girl tell the part of the story that belongs to you. It ain't your business to try to tell me and my husband's part of the story."

"But Mama Mary, everything's out in the open and there's nothing left to hide. That secret will eat you alive if you keep trying to hide it. It won't be long before she finds out, especially since she now knows that Julie is her sister," said Mom.

Mama Mary sighed again.

"Girl your granddaddy had a mean side to him. Before he fully forgave the Pastor, he called himself getting even with him by sleeping 'round with his daughter. Those two chullen belongs to your granddaddy. The bas**** wasn't a lick of good," Mama Mary said with conviction.

I was speechless. Literally speechless. I sat there for about ten minutes, and I begin to cry Not because I was sad but because I felt sorry for all of these Christians who felt the need to lie to maintain their image. I had to wonder if they were convinced that Jesus could help, that this wasn't too hard for God.

I felt sorry for them because I begin to think that all of these years of going to church was just routine. Did they know how to draw on God's power? In this hour I knew that we needed to pray, so I broke my silence by asking them to join me in prayer.

After prayer, I told my mother and grandmother that I didn't hold anything against them. I told them that I wanted them to get their relationship right with Jesus.

I expected Mama Mary to reply by asking me what makes me think that her relationship with Jesus ain't right, but she didn't. Instead, she replied by saying, "thank you baby."

She was thanking me for being an example of forgiveness, courage, and commitment.

"You know I have to repent. There was so much wrong that I participated in, concerning this situation. I walked around with bitterness in my heart for my husband, but I took it out on the Pastor, rather than talk to through it with my husband. I felt if the Pastor would not have slept with our daughter then my husband would not have had a relationship with his. Truth is, we never gave Pastor Johnson a real chance to be a father to you. That wasn't fair to either of y'all. It was downright selfish. Your mama and his were together before he surrendered his life to Christ, but he wasn't a bad even before then. Him and your mama were both young and we tried to pressure them into marriage. He just wouldn't allow us to control him like that.

I can sit here for the rest of my life and say that it was his fault that my husband did what he did, but the truth is, my husband did that because he allowed his flesh to control him. He was saved, but he needed to be sanctified. In order to keep folks from talking about us, I did everything I could to make the Pastor look bad. Doing that was easier than dealing with the mess my husband had made at our own house. I know we've seen many Pastors in error, but there's a lot going on that Pastors are not even aware of. There's also a lot going on that the Pastor has addressed without us knowing that it was addressed. He was going to have my husband step down from being a deacon, but I asked him not to do it. He was kind to me although I have been mean to him. I could have handled it very different.

He's waiting to ask you for forgiveness. He wants to make it right with you and with Julie. He feels that he should not have given up so easily. I've asked him to forgive me and he told me that he already had. Next Sunday me and your mama will be returning to church.

Julie is your sister, so I have to find it in my heart to forgive her. I'm going to make an effort to do so. I believe that God has forgiven me so how dare I hold something against someone else. There's no need in me spending the last of my days holding on to what I can't change. You let her know that she and her children are welcome over here. No need in them having to suffer as a result of our mess."

I hugged Mama Mary real tight. I didn't say anything because she already knew that my hug meant that everything was okay.

That Sunday was a very defining moment in my life. There were so many lessons in what was revealed to me that day. Julie was shocked yet excited to find out that we were sisters. She knew she had someone on her side who she could depend on. She apologized to Mama Mary and we all know it was sincere.

Mama Mary was glad to accept Julie and her children.

Pastor Johnson understood that we probably would not be calling him daddy, but it was a blessing to know that he was. We agreed to have Sunday dinner together once a month. Me, him,

Julie, and my nieces. His wife and other children still needed more time, and that was understandable. This was a lot.

Chapter Highlights:

The statement The Doors of the Church are open has become very misleading because many have accepted the call to the altar for the outward appearance but not for the inward transformation. Nowadays the open doors of the church seem to have less to do with having people commit to Jesus and more to do with increasing membership.

Some churches will highlight how many members they have, but it should be asked, "of that number, how many have you converted into disciples of Jesus Christ?"

The doors of the church should be open to peace, yet it has been opened to turmoil.

The doors of the church should be open to singing praises to God, yet it has been open to slandering the name of our Pastors and church leaders.

The doors of the church should be open to integrity, yet it has been opened to protecting images.

The doors of the church should be open to faith, yet it has been opened to foolishness.

CHAPTER 6

A connection with God is a common reason why people go to church. Those who have accepted Jesus Christ as Lord and Savior find that going to church is a way to practice their Christian faith.

Surveys have revealed reasons why people say they attend church to include, being closer to God, church provides a spiritual foundation for their children, church helps them to become a better person, and they find comfort during their times of trouble. Valuable sermons and being a part of a community of faith are also reasons for attending church.

It is a common American belief that not attending church signifies a lack of faith, unbelief, or a sinful life; however, this is not always true. There are many believers who stopped attending church because of a bad church experience.

Some believe that their faith can be expressed in other ways. With the decline of church attendance on the rise, the need for evangelism is greater. People need to be loved back to fellowship and not shamed and judged. The decline in church attendance is not just unbelievers. There are many Christians who are throwing in the towels on church. Because of this decline may could think that it is the fault of the church. Why are people not coming? Some say that they don't feel welcome when they do attend. The church can't continue to conclude that non-attendance means non-belief. The church has to figure out how to guard the hearts of those who have been let down. Those who have experienced church hurt must be convinced that they should renew their commitment to Jesus Christ.

Feeling connected and whole, the feeling of having emotional support, the opportunity to express gratitude to God, a chance to find a deeper meaning for life, are all benefits of attending church.

No one should have to experience a nasty attitude from a church usher.

No one should be asked to move to the back of a church they are visiting because there is respect of persons at that church and the "important people" sit in the front.

No one should have to be led by a Pastor who has a wife and several side chicks.

No one should have to belong to a church where they faithfully tithe and give offerings but are told no when they find themselves in need.

No one should serve faithfully at a church that won't even buy a cupcake from them.

Yet, these are some of the things that Christians are experiencing in their church. These are some of the things that are making people feel content with staying in the bed on Sunday morning.

There is an obvious lack of Christ-committed individuals who are running the church and attending the church.

Commitment is evident when seeking the glory of God for the good of ALL is the focus. Church leaders should not be on a popularity binge while seeking to bring honor to themselves. Church attenders should stop internalizing every bad experience and calling it quits when they are offended. This is bigger than us.

Commitment is evident when there is unconditional love displayed. The church and the church attenders both should vow to love like Jesus. There should be a mutual understanding that when the church finds out that someone has been overtaken in a fault, that they find ways to restore them and not write them off. Likewise, church attenders have to be cognizant that they are dealing with humans so things won't always be flawless. As long as repentance and a willingness to correct behavior is present, then that is reason enough to stay connected with the church.

Commitment is evident when discipleship is a priority. There must be some practiced loyalty to Jesus, not some promised loyalty. It can be promised, but it's not effective if it's not practiced. The loyalty from a disciple holds up under pressure. The spirits of Peter and Judas, denial and betrayal, does not creep in when there is commitment. The committed church will disciple all who want to be discipled. Maturing individuals and allowing them to use their gifts are not just limited to the "inner circle" or the Pastor's "VIP" list. As such, church attenders should be willing to be used and to serve before they accuse the church of not discipling them.

If you have ever been hurt in church, then you know exactly how traumatic such an experience can be. Not only can it cause substantial emotional damage, church hurt can be deeply disorienting and can cause you to feel like Christ has abandoned you. But did you know that you can overcome church hurt and find strength to go on? When you are committed to Christ, His unconditional love provides healing and empowerment.

No matter what the doors of the church opens up to, if you enter in for love, healing, compassion, and service, you will find it all in Jesus.

The Doors of the church are open, I found someone to rescue me.

When The Doors of the church opened, I found Jesus and He has set me free!

Pamela D. Smith

Pamela D. Smith

60

Pamela D. Smith

60

ABOUT THE AUTHOR

Encouraging, Equipping & Empowering women and teens to align their spirituality with their success goals so that their lives are peaceful, purposeful, and productive is the mission of this inspirational evangelist. "Enriching women in such a way so that 'I am good because I am God's' becomes their mantra is my life's assignment," says Pamela D. Smith.

This Evangelist, International Life Coach & Speaker, Author, and Self-Publishing Consultant has dedicated her diverse pursuits to elevating the spiritual lives of women around the world. Born in Northern Louisiana and now residing in Arlington, Texas-she is affectionately known as the "Prayer Plug" to many. It is through fervent prayer that she has created a multifaceted ministry that connects with people through a plethora of platforms and projects. Such would include the release of a prayer cd, **Quiet Time to Pray**, and a Life Enrichment Ministry titled, **Go(o)d Girl**. This ministry empowers women to embrace their spiritual and physical attributes and to engulf themselves in God's word so that the person aligns with the purpose. Pamela has self-published some women empowerment life coaching books titled: **E3:**

Encouraged, Equipped, Empowered and *Life, Love, Liberty: A 21-Day Spiritual Life Coaching Journey.*

In addition to *Inwardly: The Set Free Life,* she's also published a prayer journal: *Quiet Time to Pray* and a family book collaboration, *Dear Go(o)d Girl.* Pamela has been featured on *The Sharvette Mitchell* blog radio show, *Diva Talk* blog radio, *The Authors Show, Jubilee Magazine, Elite Magazine, Glambitious Online, Jazzy Creative Magazine, Dallas Voyage* and *Sheen Magazine.com.* She was a 2017 Pink Carpet Honoree at **LaShae's** Business Women Expo. Having an undergraduate degree in Social Science and a Master's degree in Business Management, Pamela will soon channel her business savvy into additional efforts. As a self-publishing consultant, she assists authors with publishing and marketing their work and she teaches them how to use their book to build their brand. Additionally, her services that include preaching, teaching, life-coaching, consulting, keynote speaking, panel speaking, and workshop facilitating; will continue to help pave her road of success as a ministry maven.

Pamela's first ministry is within her own home. She is married to Randall R. Smith, Sr. and is the mother of three sons.

Connect with Pamela on Instagram @pameladenisesmith and @rpsmithllc or visit the website at www.rpsmiths.com